NATURE CALLS

by

E. R. Bills

May 2023

STARKWEATHER IMPRINTS

it's funny
but it's true
and it's true
but it's not funny

Daniel Johnston
"Some Things Last A Long Time"

1

Raul Najera was a serious young man. He had lived in the Kermit area of West Texas all his life, and the only reason he took a job at the Andrews County Nuclear Waste Authority was to leak the goings on behind the storage facility's heavily fortified walls. The Nuclear Waste Authority (NWA) had applied for another permit to dump radioactive materials near Kent, and Najera had family in nearby Van Horn. The NWA had promised to pay for a new school and a state-of-the-art football stadium and track in Van Horn if the dwindling community signed off on the project. So far, Van Horn had balked.

On this particular nightshift, Najera and another employee, Doogie Ross, were walking the perimeter of the facility, taking a long smoke break. They strolled away from the front gate, toward the first corner to the south.

"You ever been over here in the daytime?" Ross asked, zig-zagging his flashlight along the ground.

"No," Najera replied. "Not since I applied."

Ross smoke and dipped. Najera didn't even drink coffee. Their walks outside the NWA walls were just a break from the stultifying routine. Najera felt like a prison guard on the midnight shift. Except nothing in the "penitentiary" was alive, much less penitent. The term radioactive, though. Was an active ingredient really dead?

"Well," Ross said, lighting up. "I've lived all over Texas and one thing every place in Texas definitely has, is fire ants. Fucking fire ants everywhere." Ross spit, using his flashlight hand to track the gob's landing, and then, took a long drag. "Not here, though," he continued, gesturing expansively with his cigarette hand. "And that's weird, right? It's like they sense what's here. It's like they know."

"They may be smarter than we think," Najera replied. "It makes you wonder."

"It does. But it's damn good money. Hell, I was working fast food at Taco Vato's before I landed this gravy train. Now, I'm drivin' a King Ranch."

Something moved in the darkness beyond the perimeter lighting that wilted outside the facility walls. Ross swung his flashlight in its direction. "Did you hear that?" he rasped.

"No," Najera replied. "What was it?"

But they both heard it now, out past a clump of stubborn desert shrub. Ross flicked his cigarette away. It bounced and rolled in the uneven sand.

A low clicking and scuttling sound filled the air, and it was getting louder.

"What the hell is that?" Ross said. "I—"

By the time Ross trained his flashlight on the approaching creature, it was too late. It caught him in an instant, and Najera ran. The light from Ross' fallen flashlight lit Najera's path.

The thing looked like something from those Pokemon cards Najera collected as a kid, a *Venipede* or a *Whirlipede*—but he didn't stick around to see how accurately it compared to his childhood memories.

This was his first full sprint since junior college, but he was long-striding now, trying to remind himself to breathe. For a moment, he thought he might make it, but the clicking, like the sound of his heart, grew loud. Right when he thought his chest might burst from the pressure, the thing was upon him.

2

Treat Kearny's friends called him "Tree," because he was tall and rangy, crowding most doorways and an imposing figure in the hall outside his classroom. He taught Latin at L.D. Bell High School in Hurst, Texas, and was as amicable as he was huge.

Sitting Indian style in his eight-man tent (a two-man tent was much too small and a four-man tent was still something of a squeeze), grading papers by lantern light, he lamented getting such a late start.

A few years back, a group of Germans had purchased the abandoned ghost town of Lobo sixteen miles south of Van Horn on US-90. Every other summer they staged the Desert Dust Film Festival at a converted gas station and abandoned hotel. This year they were holding the event in late fall, over Thanksgiving break, the long weekend after the holiday. The Germans held a similar harvest celebration in early October. They called it *Erntedankfest*.

Treat had met one of the Germans at a hostel in Prague several years before, and this would be his second festival attendance. He was eager to see his European friends, but slow to get away after a Thanksgiving visit with his family in Dallas. His delayed departure put him in Odessa around 11 p.m. and, just after 12:20 a.m., he decided to stop in Kent. Kent was also a ghost town, located about an hour-and-a-half east of Van Horn. He decided to pitch his tent there by headlight, behind the shell of the abandoned schoolhouse on State Hwy 118, just south of I-10. He liked the windowless façade of the old rust-brick schoolhouse in daylight. It was picturesque, a mark of civilization against indomitable, frontier desolation— what Latin used to be in the old days. The tent smelled vaguely of Deep Woods Off, but there were no mosquitoes in that part of Texas in late fall.

At around 2 a.m. he put his red pen down and decided to call it a night. First, however, nature called. He unzipped the tent entrance and slipped outside. He stepped off about twenty paces to relieve himself and stared into the cloudless night sky. He could see millions of stars and the low, glowing curve of the Milky Way perpendicular to the far horizon.

As he unbuttoned and unzipped his cargo shorts, he heard something. A clicking, and then a scuttling. He spotted something moving low and fast about fifty yards out. The clicking and scuttling got louder as he turned, holding up his shorts, and ran. But it was too late.

He only screamed once.

3

Annette Carden was finally getting used to Texas.

Originally from Colorado, Carden attended college at Oregon State. Neither locale was especially useful in terms of her degree, entomology—the study of insects. But her specialty was centipedes and millipedes, and, broken down further, the phylum Myriapoda. Carden was on a tenure track at Texas Tech University, West Texas being one of the best places to study Myriapods and the perfect habitat for her favorite, millipede diplopods known as *Orthoporus ornatus*. They looked like thick earthworms, except they had legs. Hundreds of them. And, after a heavy rain in far West Texas, thousands attempted to cross state roads and highways in search of new places to burrow.

Carden spent her summers in the Big Bend area and, this year, her Thanksgiving break. After a rough semester, a trip home to Colorado held little appeal. More than family time, she needed to decompress. To Carden, Texas was becoming startlingly medieval for women and education, and especially science. Perhaps, after receiving tenure, she might move on. For now, however, she was going to relax at her place near the Christmas Mountains.

That was where the deputy sheriff found her.

Carden kept a decent little getaway cabin on a sandy, five-acre lot in the Terlingua Ranch Estates. Very few Ranch residents had power, because the waspish inhabitants refused to agree on or mutually concede to power company easements in their dusty refuge from cellphone reception, traffic and on-the-grid accoutrements. Carden had water delivered to her 1,000-gallon, ground-mounted water tank during her summer residency, and the cottage's metal roof was neatly corralled by a gutter that emptied into a separate, 500-gallon rain storage tank. She got her power from a combination of solar panels, a wind turbine and, as a last resort, a diesel generator, slab-mounted, with its own ventilated shed-like structure. She also had propane gas delivered for cooking and some heating. She took solar showers in summer, but relied on the trailer's tankless, 120V instahot water heater in the cooler months. The locals kept to themselves and she didn't get many visitors. So, when she spotted a vehicle stirring up dust on her long gravel drive, she was slightly alarmed. Then she saw the red and blue flashers.

The cruiser pulled up and the dust settled. A Culberson County sheriff's deputy, with mirror-lensed sunglasses, stepped out. He was tall and wiry, and looked to be about Carden's age.

"Hello, ma'am," he said.

"Morning, deputy. What can I do for you?"

"Are you Dr. Annette Carden?"

"I'm assistant professor Carden."

"Well, ma'am. I'm a county or so over from my jurisdiction, but we need your help."

"My help? I don't know how I could be of any help—"

"I—Dr. Carden, ma'am—it won't make any sense. We have a problem. I can try to explain it on the way over."

"Over where?"

"Kent, ma'am. North-northeast of Van Horn."

"That's a long way. I'm sorry, I don't think . . . I don't know what I could help you with."

"Can the sheriff speak with you?"

"I suppose so."

The deputy removed his sunglasses and placed them in a shirt pocket. Then he used his cell phone to call the sheriff. Carden noticed that the deputy's eyes were a light, bright blue.

"Sheriff," the deputy said, "I found her."

The deputy handed Annette the phone. The sheriff was direct and brief. They had a strange death on their hands, and they needed additional information—an expert opinion. They believed an insect may have been involved. The sheriff assured Annette that she would be compensated for her time. The deputy waited for her to get ready.

Carden wanted to take her own vehicle, but the deputy—whose last name was Therber—noted that it was best that they both took the cruiser. He could turn on the flashers and they would make better time. Traveling at speeds upwards of ninety mph, the drive would still take a while.

When they were on the road, Carden eyed the steel mesh barrier that separated the front and back seats of the cruiser. She'd never been in a police car before. Or a sheriff's department cruiser.

"What made you decide to become an "ickyologist?" Deputy Therber inquired.

"*Ickyologist?* Where'd you hear that?"

"I heard it in an Elvis movie once."

"About an Egyptian mummy at a rest home?"

"Something like that."

"*Bubba Ho-Tep?*"

"Actually, yeah. I think that was it."

"That wasn't Elvis, deputy. That was Bruce Campbell playing Elvis."

"The guy from *Evil Dead*? The original?"

"Yes, sir."

"Oh, wow. That's embarrassing. I knew I heard it somewhere. What were the bugs called?"

"Scarab beetles. They were big in Ancient Egypt, but hardly flesh-eating monsters. Scarab beetles usually subsist on dung, decaying plant material, or carrion—the flesh of dead things."

"From what I've heard about the crime scene, I'd say it was something along the lines of a scarab that dispatched our vic."

"That seems unlikely," Carden replied, shaking her head.

Deputy Therber shrugged. "If not, I guess it was something like it," he maintained.

"I can take a look," Carden said, "but my specialty is centipedes and millipedes. They're more related to Crustaceans—crabs and lobsters—than most insects. 'Bugs' aren't really part of my wheelhouse. But I might be useful in a pinch . . . pardon the pun."

"What?"

"Nothing. It's not important."

"What made you want to study that stuff?"

"Do you really want to know? Or are you just making conversation?"

"We still have a ways to go before we get to Kent. I'm interested, yes."

"Do you subscribe to evolutionary theory?"

"Evolution? I think so. From what I know about it."

"Good. That's a start."

"Oh, well. Thanks. I guess."

"I just mean that plenty of people these days still don't. It's a little scary."

"Why's that?"

"I mostly try to stay out of these discussions—but you did rouse me from the hustle and bustle of Dune Ranch."

"Is that what they call it now?"

"That's what I call it," Carden answered. "May I speak frankly?"

"I'm a fan of straight-shooters."

"Well, the fact of the matter is . . . most things in our society—our very way of life—are propped up by science . . . advanced computer technology, medical technology, transportation, mobile phones, etc. They all spring from the scientific method, which involves the formulation, applicable testing, and refinement of theory and the research and development of practical applications. Criticism is the foundation of the scientific method. Every hypothesis is open to questions and testing. If a theory doesn't hold water, it's discarded for a better one. Does it explain everything? No. But it's usually an honest attempt, and challenges are hardly forbidden—in fact, they're invited." Carden was quiet for a moment.

"The truth is," she continued, "we cling to way too many ideas that institutions refuse to allow to be challenged or questioned. Our educational system is authoritarian, but helmed by no real authorities. Just political operatives. And our political system is selectively forthcoming, and helmed by no real leaders. Just promulgators of obfuscation." Carden considered her mild harangue. It didn't seem appropriate in the cruiser, so far from the easy, predictable impudence of the faculty lounge. Maybe she belonged with all the eccentric cranks at Terlingua Ranch.

"Those opinions are chock full of ten-dollar college words I barely understand."

"Do you disagree?"

"I don't know if I know enough to disagree," Therber answered, smiling.

"That's honest."

"Well, it isn't a theory."

Carden grinned. Was he being flirtatious?

"To conclude my original point," she continued, "millipedes and centipedes are different than most insects, and actually pre-date them. My primary focus is on millipedes of the subphylum Myriapoda, but their cousins, predatory centipedes of the class Chilopoda were the first land-based predators. We're driving through an area that used to be covered by ocean. Chilopods could have evolved here 430 million years ago. Their first steps from the sea could have been taken right here."

"I think anything is possible."

"I agree. But concepts that stretch back 430 million years ago aggravate certain sensibilities, religious dogma, and cherished faith directives."

"Directives?"

"Well, we are instructed what to believe, right?"

"A fair point. I suppose I am religious," Deputy Therber said. "Religious with a dash of doubt. It seems to me that Adam and Eve weren't all that, and they certainly didn't stick the landing. And if the Big Man is all He's cracked up to be, why didn't they? It hardly made sense to me when I was younger. Now, religious faith is something I allow myself on Christmas and some holidays." Deputy Therber put his sunglasses back on. "So, you really dig this stuff?"

"I do," Carden replied. "Myriapods and Chilopods have been around as long as sharks. And coral reefs. And they'll probably be here long after we're gone."

"I don't exactly find that comforting."

"I'm not sure it thrills me, either. But it's where we find ourselves."

"It is the way you tell it. I bet you're a good teacher."

"I try. What's your first name, deputy?"
"Rodney, ma'am."
"How much farther, Rodney?"

4

When Deputy Therber and assistant professor Carden arrived at the ruins of the schoolhouse, the Sheriff and a dark-skinned DPS officer were standing out front.

As Carden stepped out of the cruiser, introductions were made. Then, the sheriff, Axil Rafferty, held forth. "I don't like this at all," he said. "Miss Carden—we wouldn't have called you out here if it wasn't absolutely necessary. I'm at a loss."

"I hope I can help, sheriff."

"Me, too, ma'am. Me, too. We have a body over there . . . or, at least parts of one. And we think—well, we don't know what to think. I'm not even sure I know what to say."

"Is it that bad?" Deputy Therber asked.

"It's pretty bad," said Rafferty. "The body is still out behind the school house . . . what's left of it anyway. And the smell. But the victim, he had something in his right hand. I wasn't sure what it was at first, but . . . well. I don't even want to think it, much less say it out loud. You should see for yourself."

The sheriff stepped around to his trunk and opened it. "I've lived out here all my life. I had an idea what this was, but I just . . . I just couldn't believe it. Who would? I couldn't process it. I needed an expert." The sheriff removed an object wrapped longways in a black contractor's trash bag. It was the shape of a slightly bent, human arm, but when the sheriff unwrapped it, it was clearly not human. It was about three feet long, dull yellow, segmented and curved, and tapered at the end, almost to a frightening point.

Carden swallowed hard.

"It almost looks like a stubby tentacle," Therber observed. "Except it's rigid."

"It feels like a giant, reinforced celery stalk," Rafferty observed. "As I said, I've lived out here forever and I think I saw something like this in a cave once. But it wasn't near this big. It was—"

"*Scolopendra Heros*," Carden suggested abruptly. "Perhaps even *Scolopendra Heros castanerceps*. With a red head. You saw it in a cave?"

"Yep," Rafferty confirmed. "Leaned over on a rock and almost placed my hand right on it."

"The head was red, the sections of the body were black, and the legs were yellowish?"

"Yes, ma'am."

"*Scolopendra Heros*. You call it the Texas redheaded centipede, the giant desert centipede, or the Devil Head centipede. It's a Chilopod."

"Like what you were talking about on the way over?" said Therber. Carden nodded without taking her eyes off the appendage.

"But these things usually don't get over six or eight inches long," Sheriff Rafferty replied. "We did find a dead one, over eighteen inches long, a year or so back. It killed a cat and then a neighbor's dog killed it. You thinking this is a leg?"

"I am. I don't like thinking it—I would need to run some tests first. I think I'm kind of in shock."

"We all are."

"You saying this came from one of those Devil's Head centipedes?" Therber asked. "The one with all the legs?"

"Devil Head. Again, it would require testing, but . . . yeah. It looks like."

"But that would mean . . . How long would that make it?"

"Forty feet," answered the DPS officer, Mateo Rios. "Give or take." Rios' eyes were dark and sharp, and wide set over a hawkish nose. He was slight, clean cut, and astute. Carden wondered if someday he wouldn't be the sheriff.

"That would make it's antennae taller than me," Rafferty replied.

"Around four stories on its hind legs," Carden said.

"But that's impossible, right?" Rafferty asked.

"It was," Carden conceded.

"Hind legs?" Therber blurted.

"Yes. In South America, they've been known to stand on their hind legs and snatch bats in midair. And I agree, sheriff. I'd guess about six feet on the antennae. Which is what they use to identify their prey. Their eyes are useless."

"I bet that's what has been getting after the hogs," Rios replied.

"Feral hogs?"

"Yes, ma'am," Officer Rios said. "We thought it might be a big mountain lion, the granddaddy of all mountain lions. Or maybe a mating pair of mountain lions come down to feed. We been finding pieces of hog carcass all over and just made the logical assumption. But this changes things."

"I'll say," Rafferty agreed.

"That would explain how mangled the hog carcasses have been," Rios added, "and the smell."

"The *Heros* is venomous, and the venom is neurotoxic. The toxin it injects is pretty potent, and possibly deadly for any small mammal out here. And for a *Heros* that size, it would include feral hogs and mammals of the human variety. And, yes, it would rot the remains in a different way. Accelerated necrosis. Nasty stuff."

"That's what was weird," Rios replied. "Finding pieces of hog with no buzzards around."

"We found the leg of this thing in the hand of the man it attacked," said Rafferty. "He was a big dude."

"He never had a chance," replied Carden. "Devil Head centipedes are aggressive and fast. They usually attack other invertebrates or small vertebrates, including small mammals, reptiles, and amphibians. But one that big . . ."

5

Sheriff Rafferty had been right. There wasn't much left of Treat Kearny, especially intact. Blood, entrails, shit, strips of skin and shards of bone. But they found his wallet in the tent. Besides that, a striated length of Kearney's leg, a strip of red-haired sideburn (or pubic hair), the right hand that had grabbed and held onto the creature's leg, and his entire left arm, which featured a tattoo of the Orion constellation on the interior wrist. Officer Rios held up a pair of bloody cargo shorts with a short stick.

It was difficult for Carden to micro-extrapolate the macro evidence, but she tried and took another look at the *Heros* appendage. Therber stood alongside, and Sheriff Rafferty nodded into his flip phone. "Yep," he said. "Uh-huh. What time you think? Okay. I'll get back to you." Rafferty's face seemed to lose its color.

There was an unreality to the entire crime scene, which made Carden wonder if it could even be called a crime scene. Could anything in the natural world, besides man or humankind, be considered criminal? She didn't get to reflect on the point very long.

"I think there's another one," Rafferty said. "At the Texas-New Mexico border, near the NWA facility."

"But that's a hundred miles away," Officer Rios replied.

"Where?" Carden inquired.

"Near a nuclear waste storage facility out there in Andrews County. Two more victims. Sounds like the same M.O."

"North of Kermit," Deputy Therber added.

"Kermit, Wink, Mentone . . ." Carden mumbled.

"What did you tell them?" Rios asked.

"Nothing," Rafferty barked. "What do we really know?"

"That place was originally restricted to the monitored storage of low-grade, radioactive material," Therber said. "But I heard they fast-tracked a broader application to accept more hazardous stuff."

"I heard that, too," said Rios. "Nuclear waste with half-lives lasting thousands of years."

"That's why the citizens of Van Horn were fighting plans for a second facility," Rafferty replied. "We didn't want that crap in our back yard."

"What if it's led . . ." Carden hesitated. "That might explain . . ." Carden's entire person stiffened.

"What?" Deputy Therber said. "What is it?"

Carden mulled it over and finally said it. "What if this giant Devil Head Chilopod is the result of an NWA leak or ground exposure?"

"That's a hundred miles away," Rios repeated. "Could something like whatever that thing is move that far in a night?"

"It's not impossible," Carden answered.

"Wait," Therber said, taking a step. "Dr. Carden, wait a minute. Do you really expect us to believe the goddamn King Kong of centipedes is hot-rodding around West Texas, mowing people down?"

"I wouldn't put it quite like that, Rodney," Carden said. "But, yes. It's possible. You saw the appendage in the sheriff's trunk." The sheriff noted Carden's use of Therber's first name.

"I did," Therber replied. "I know. But this is B-movie science-fiction stuff. *Ickyology.* You know that, right?"

Carden pointed at the dull yellow appendage and answered Therber with raised eyebrows.

Rafferty turned to Officer Rios. "You have a good map of this area?"

"I do."

"Could you grab it for me and bring it over to the hood of my cruiser?"

"I can, Sheriff. I will."

6

Carden spelled it out slowly.

"They've found record-breaking, giant millipede fossils that were six feet long and probably weighed over a hundred pounds. As I told Deputy Therber on the ride over, millipedes and centipedes were some of the first creatures to ply dry, solid ground; they were the first land predators and hunters. And that isn't the stuff of 50s B-movie sci-fi. Those are the facts. But speaking of the 50s, has anyone ever heard of the Bikini Atoll?"

"Girls skinny-dipping at Balmorhea in the old days," Therber joked, trying to be clever. "With no bikini at all."

Carden ignored him. "The Bikini Atoll in the Pacific Ocean is where the United States conducted multiple early nuclear tests. We detonated over two dozen nuclear bombs there, all told, and today, even after almost seventy years, dangerous levels of radiation still permeate every biological property in the area. Strontium 19. Genetic mutations. Decreased longevity. Sharks with strange fin configurations, invertebrates that are growing larger. And growing larger faster."

"Sweet Jesus," Sheriff Rafferty said.

"Yes," Carden replied. "I'm not stating anything for the record. But a Chilopod exposed to radiation? It could produce a mutation like this. I know it's sounds like 'Godzilla' stuff. Except in Mr. Kearney's case, if this was a giant Chilopod, sorry— he was Japan."

Officer Rios walked back up with the maps. They spread one out on the hood of the sheriff's cruiser and Rafferty studied it. "A hundred miles in a night," he said.

"It's not impossible," Therber replied. "The Comanche could do three hundred a night on horseback."

"It would be feasible, for sure," Carden said. "*Heros* are nocturnal, so it'd probably stay away from the highway and travel in remote areas, away from light. But we're getting ahead of ourselves. How long has that nuclear waste facility been there? This may not be some spontaneous anomaly. It may be the accelerated evolution of an organism over a period of years."

"That doesn't help," Rafferty complained. "In fact, that makes my asshole pucker. Where do you think it'd go next?"

"I couldn't answer that with any real certainty," Carden conceded. "But where's the next big town? Especially one that might be approached in the dark?"

"Van Horn," Therber replied. "Population right at or just under two thousand, but the biggest place for practically a hundred miles in any direction."

"Are there any goat or horse ranches in the area?" Rafferty inquired. "Where are you finding the hog remains?"

"The outskirts of Van Horn," Officer Rios replied. "And there are seven or eight goat ranches."

"That might be a good place to start," Carden said. "It's finding food near light, or on the edge of lighted areas. Van Horn might be a good spot to check, especially before it gets dark."

"Should we call in the cavalry?" Therber asked.

The sheriff grabbed the map and started rolling it up.

"Maybe a chopper?" suggested Rios.

"The professor said they were nocturnal," Rafferty replied. "A chopper wouldn't do us much good at night, would it?"

"Probably not."

"And, besides, what would you tell the chopper crew we were looking for?"

Rios smiled grimly. "Roger that."

"It's a guessing game," Rafferty said. "And I like the professor's instincts."

"You think it's heading west?"

"So far, it has."

"What about the highway?"

"It had to cross it to get here. And there are probably sixteen bridges and underpasses between here and Van Horn."

"That's right," Rios observed. "Should we release the information to the public?"

"I don't think so," said Rafferty. "I think it's a bad idea."

"Afraid people will panic?"

"Not at all," Rafferty replied. "People out here don't panic easy. But if the people know, the government might know. Or find out."

"And? What are you saying?" Therber asked.

"I'm talking out of turn," Rafferty replied. "But the government's patrons are making billions of dollars dumping radioactive garbage from all over North America at NWA—shitting where we eat, so-to-speak. Hell, there may be more money in that than there is in oil and gas. And definitely easier money. I think they'd swoop in and cover this up. Change the narrative. People might even disappear. Money talks, and obscene money—the kind of money we're talking about—stalks, always on the look out for threats. I'd like to avoid finding myself in their crosshairs. And this little chilidog jailbreak would give them the perfect excuse to cover all this shit up."

"Chilopod," Carden corrected.

"Yes," Rafferty said. "Chilopod. I meant Chilopod."

"Well," Carden wryly observed, "It seems counterintuitive, but I think Sheriff Rafferty is right. That's exactly how it might play out."

"So what do we do?" Therber asked.

"Reach out to whoever you know you can trust and really count on," Rafferty advised. "Contact anybody you'd take a bullet for. Bring them in on the down-low, and on a need-to-know basis, only. We'll try to corner this thing and kill it. Be done with it."

"Kill it with what?" Rios inquired.

"M4 rifles," Therber suggested.

"We have some back at the office and even more at Van Horn PD," Rafferty said. "And some at the local gun shops. Buy 'em out, guns and ammo."

"But what do we tell them?"

"I don't give a shit," Rafferty replied. "Tell 'em it's for a raffle. Say it's to help protect the border."

Rios rolled his eyes.

7

Rios grabbed the M4s and some ammo, and picked up an off-duty Border Security officer he was old friends with. Rafferty enlisted his son, who was home for the weekend from Angelo State. Carden stuck with Deputy Therber. They headed to Fort Davis, Rafferty to Van Horn, and Rios, eventually, due north on State Highway 54, toward the Guadalupe Mountains.

Rafferty was possessed of an increasing sense of dread, but he kept things as light as he could with his son, Harwood.

"Sounds pretty farfetched to me, Sheriff," Harwood said, with a playful smirk. "You guys must really be getting bored."

"I hope you're right, meathead. Believe me, nothing would make me happier. I hope it's a wild goose chase."

"I'm kidding. Nothing surprises me anymore. The crap these days," Harwood said. "You think it can't get any weirder, but it does. Nothing seems set in stone anymore, like it's real or the only thing that's real."

"I hear ya—I really do. It's the truth. It seems like it's coming from all sides, even out here. But we can't curl up in a little ball. We gotta keep our shoulder to it and keep going."

"I know, I know. Hell or high water. I don't need a lecture."

"I know that, son. I'm well aware. I don't mean to . . . I wish you'd have picked another weekend to come home. Your mom and I are always happy to see you, but what's happening today—of all days—it's Twilight Zone stuff. It worries me. I hope it's a lark."

"Meadowlark Lemon," Harwood replied.

"*Meadowlark Lemon,*" Rafferty repeated. "I can't believe you remember him, kiddo. That slays me. I haven't thought of him since—sheesh, I can't remember when. I'm impressed." Rafferty's sudden enthusiasm waned. "Thing is, we may need some of Meadowlark's moves if we run into this thing. I really just brought you along to man the radio. If things get out of hand, I want you to stay in the cruiser."

"I'm a decent shot. You know that."

"I do know that. But I don't know what we're looking at here. And we'll have plenty of guns. But if things get cattywampus, get on the radio. Stay put and call in the reinforcements. Your mama would skin me alive if something happened to you."

8

Rios liked the drive to the Guads. The Delaware Mountains to the east and the Sierra Diablos Range to the west. His buddy Paco was a fan as well. Paco's father, who left him and his mother early on, was full-blood Apache, and he talked about how his great-great grandfather had snuck off to the Guads for ceremonies even after they settled on the reservations. The Guadalupe Mountains were sacred to them.

Paco was younger than Rios, but solid in the ways that counted. He was tough, practical, and kept things in perspective. Rios liked him. Family ties were important, but bonds of reliance mattered, too. Especially under fire. Under a microscope. Under extreme duress. A lot of Rios' law enforcement colleagues didn't have that kind of commitment. Paco was reliable. And he didn't make a habit of being up to things he shouldn't. Neither of them bought into the "Back the Badge" bullshit, or "Blue Lives Matter." If you did your job and did it right, and did it honest, you were the badge. And you didn't need to win any popularity contests or become political pawns. That's how Rios saw it, anyway.

"I'd love to have me a little hacienda out here someday," Paco said, "but I'll never be able to afford it. Bezos is a *pendejo*. Fucking 10,000-year clock, my ass."

"They say he owns half the Diablos," Rios replied.

"I know. To build a clock that ticks once a year."

"The 'Clock of the Long Now.'"

"Is that what they call it?"

"It is. They have two small prototypes, one in California and one in Europe. But the big one ought to come on line in the next few years."

"What's the point of it? Why put it out here?"

"I have no idea why they decided to do it out here, outside of the fact that there's nothing out here and maybe it was cheaper to buy half a mountain range here."

"Again, though. Why?"

"They say they're doing it to make us think differently about time, to think more long-term."

"That's funny," Paco said. "They took this land from people that thought seven generations ahead, and they didn't need a fancy clock built in a mountain to do it."

Rios nodded. "I hear the hour or 'century' hand will advance every one hundred years. And they say a cuckoo will come out when the clock strikes a new millennium."

"Ain't that some shit," Paco sighed. *"Pinches gringos."*

"Pinches gringos," Rios repeated.

"So. You think we'll find this . . . this whatever it is thing?"

"I'm not so sure," Rios replied. "It may not be that simple, anyway. This whole thing is crazy, a precautionary measure at best. Which is probably smart. But we're not exactly sure what it is or if we'll be able to find it."

"Is it just us greasers?" Paco inquired with a playful grin. "Or will Raff and Ponyboy be packing?"

"Rafferty has been around," Rios replied. Don't underestimate him. And Therber is no slouch. He's got some cactus to him when it counts."

"Good. Then, I guess we're set," Paco remarked. "Been awhile since I carried an M4 carbine. Seems heavy. And it can do some heavy damage." Paco grinned. "It wouldn't hurt to come home a hero, though. I hear your sister is graduating from New Mexico State soon."

"It'd be hard to call on her with an M4 stuck up your ass," Rios said.

"I'll keep that in mind," Paco replied. "It would definitely make it harder to aim."

Rios laughed and Paco flashed another big grin. "You always were too uptight, bro."

"Just be ready," Rios said. "We may not see anything. We probably won't see anything."

9

Carden and Therber shot west across State Highway 166, took the jog on CR 505, and headed north toward Van Horn on US-90.

Biological imperative, Carden thought.

Not in terms of the *Scolopendra Heros*, but Deputy Therber. He was lithe and handsome, not exactly Pinot Grigio, but what they said in the movies about handsome men in this part of the world: a long, cool glass of water. And she was feeling thirsty.

Was it the abrupt, wild, surreal quality of the entire day, or the crazy, half-baked plan they were now engaged in? *Was danger an aphrodisiac?*

"Peso for your thoughts," Therber said.

"What?" Carden said. "Oh. Thanks. I was just thinking."

"That's what I said."

"Oh, yeah. Right."

"About what?"

Carden lied. "About how this wasn't how I planned to spend my day."

Therber smiled. "Yeah, I thought about dropping you off in Fort Davis and trying to arrange for someone else to take you home. I mean . . . if you wanted to sit this one out. For the record, though, I'm glad you came."

It was Carden's turn to smile.

"Now, don't get me wrong," Therber continued. "I truly really do hope you're wrong. About all of it. Because, well, if you're not . . . hell, then I don't know when or how this all ends."

"I hope I'm wrong, too," Carden said. "But you saw that appendage."

"You ever seen anything like that before?"

"No. Nothing even close."

Therber drove for a while in silence, clearly chewing on something in his mind. "If it is what we think it might be, could this thing be a one-off? How do they . . . ? Do they lay eggs?"

"Yes," Carden said.

"Shit."

"But there's a good chance it's a one-off," Carden added. "A Frankenstein, of sorts. A sterile mutation. The kiss of extinction."

"Beg your pardon?"

"A dominant sterile or dominant lethal mutation," Carden explained. "They're often short-lived, so they wouldn't qualify for natural selection."

"The losing-est lottery ticket in the world," Therber said. "One and done."

"Exactly. And that would work in our favor."

"We'd just have to stop the one."

After they passed through Valentine, they soon saw the participants of the Desert Dust Film Festival on their left.

"What are they doing?" asked Carden.

"Some kind of desert hipster concert or carnival or something."

"Do you think they're in danger?"

"I don't know what to think," Therber admitted.

"Where are you from?"

"Juno."

"*Juno*. Like the movie?"

"Movie?"

"J-U-N-O."

"Well, it's spelled the same. But Juno is a ghost town now, southeast of here, in Val Verde County. Not too far from the Devil's River."

Carden shook her head. "Is there anything out here that isn't named after something ominous?"

"It's not like that freaky beetle of yours, professor," Therber replied, grinning. "In what we refer to out here, in ten-dollar college words, it's a misnomer. The Devil's River may be the prettiest place in Texas. It's just really hard to get to."

"Well," Carden said, raising her eyebrows. "Once we get done with this monster hunt, maybe you could take your professor friend out there one day.”

“Maybe.”

“I’d like that, I think.”

“Me, too. I think. It would beat chasing a 100-legged freak all over creation.”

Carden grew pensive for a moment. “That must be strange, coming from a place that no longer exists. A ghost town.”

Therber grinned. “It’s a lot like coming from a small town—that died.”

“I’m serious.”

“Well, Professor Carden. Since you asked. Life out here . . . it appears and disappears, and sometimes reappears. The places are like lightning bugs. They blink in and out. Communities pop up, collapse and vanish. There are cities on current maps where no one even lives now. People always come to build a future for themselves, but sometimes they don’t last. You look away for a minute, and they’re gone. They’re somewhere else. But never for very long.”

“Is that what the sheriff meant earlier, about the people who live out here?”

"Close enough, I suppose. There are easier places to be, for sure."

"Why do you stay?"

Therber gave her a funny glance. "I like chasing fireflies." He grinned, again. "I keep an empty jar in the trunk."

"With holes in the lid?"

"Of course."

They were both enjoying this and they knew it.

Then, they got the call.

10

When they arrived, Rios' cruiser was upside down on the north side of US-180, about fifteen yards into the salt basin that sat on the western edge of the base of El Capitan, the southernmost tip of the Guadalupe Mountains. The cruiser's air bags had deployed and Rios and Paco suffered only minor injuries, which Harwood was treating with a standard first aid kit from Rafferty's vehicle.

Rios was heading west on 180 when the creature attempted to cross the asphalt in a hurry just ahead of him. Going about 70 mph, the cruiser T-boned the Devil Head and flipped, rolling twice. The Devil Head survived, but only long enough to drag its near-severed mid-section over to the south side of the road and down into a dry gully.

It probably wouldn't have mattered, but Rios hadn't exactly been watching the road. Just east of the site of the collision, there was an old, abandoned adobe brick motel on the north side of US-180. Rios remembered staying there when he was young, but now it was just a collapsing ruin, filled with trash and pocked with tourist graffiti. He always checked it out when he passed by.

Paco was sitting off the shoulder, on the north side of 180. Except for some wicked contusions, he seemed to be in a surprised daze. Rios had a cut over his right eye and a sprained wrist. The creature had gotten the worst of it.

"I guess an exoskeleton is no match for Detroit steel," Sheriff Rafferty said. "Y'all were lucky." The sheriff already had a semi with a trailer and a backhoe on the way, and he was putting on a good face. But he was troubled. This is how it's going to start, he thought. Rafferty didn't know what the story was, or how it would end, but he knew this was how it would start. And he suddenly wanted to be someplace else, maybe Abilene or Fort Worth. Maybe San Angelo, closer to Harwood.

Sheriff Rafferty had a bone-deep suspicion that he didn't understand anything and that he would never understand anything. The unreality of the creature, the sections of what he considered its elongated abdomen torn, and guts splashed and stinking. It was freakish and hardly seemed earthly.

Did insects even have hearts?

Did they have brains?

He'd never thought about it before. And he'd always heard they would be here long after humans were gone.

Was that why?

11

Carden stood stock still, dumbfounded. Deputy Therber checked on Officer Rios and helped Paco to his feet.

"Is it dead?" Paco asked. "It's not still alive, is it?"

"No, it's not," said Therber. "It's gone. Are you okay?"

"I'm okay. I . . . I just can't believe . . . *What the fuck is that thing?* I've never seen anything like it."

"Me, neither, amigo. Me, neither."

Deputy Therber and Sheriff Rafferty walked over to Carden.

"We should bury it," Rafferty said. "I got a truck and a backhoe on the way."

"You don't think," Carden trailed off, "we should tell someone?"

"No. Absolutely not. If we do, there'll be men in black here tomorrow. You think they'll let this be? What was it Winston Churchill said? Never waste a disaster. This will open the door. They'll come in under the pretense of cleaning this up, but they'll stay to clean up . . . in terms of their pocketbooks. That other nuclear waste dump will be a done deal. They'll cover all this up. And they may cover us up, too."

Carden crossed her arms. "I'd like to say I could argue that point with serious conviction. But I can't."

"I say we don't give them the chance," Rafferty said. "I think it's our only chance."

Carden turned to Rodney. "What do you think, Deputy Therber?"

"I think this is a big fucking Devil Head kiddie train," Therber said. "With several cars and a caboose. And if it becomes a thing, it really will be the insects' turn."

"And we'll have brought it on ourselves," Carden stated unequivocally. "What if we got a television station out here? What if we got it to the press?"

"The nearest station is in El Paso . . . or Fort Stockton . . ."

"How long you think it would take them to get out here, sheriff?"

"A while, but they might beat the truck. What do we tell them to get them out here?"

"Tell them it's a cartel massacre," Therber suggested. "Bodies everywhere, kids, puppy dogs . . . they'll come runnin'. Offer them the scoop, but tell them to keep it hush-hush."

The three hiked up the sandy incline to 180. Rios and Paco were leaning on the sheriff's cruiser.

"Where's Harwood?" Rafferty asked.

"He went to take a leak," Rios answered.

Rafferty got on the phone and called KASO, in El Paso. It was just starting to get dark.

12

It didn't even look real, Harwood thought. Almost like a bad CGI effect. But alien. If there'd been any cellphone reception out there, he'd have sent a picture.

Just as he finished relieving himself and started to button up his Levis, Harwood felt the earth move under his feet and stumbled backward. The walls of the old adobe motel shook and began collapsing.

Harwood heard a loud clicking, and then a rumble. He backed up two or three steps and then turned and started to run. "Dad!" he screamed, "Dad!"

Rafferty turned and dropped his phone.

He didn't have time to react.

An enormous, 747-sized centipede with a dragon-red head and a thousand dull, yellow legs smashed through the ruins of the adobe motel and suddenly dwarfed Harwood, front pincers scissoring him to bits without even slowing down.

The sheriff howled gutturally, drew his pistol and started firing into the ghastly scarlet hellspawn's approaching, beaky face. The creature's impossibly long antennae cut telephone lines as it surmounted US-180 and immediately began wreaking havoc on the cruisers and their defenders. Paco reacted first, spraying the creature with an M4, and everyone else except Carden emptied their weapons.

But to no avail.

The gigantic, seemingly horned Devil Head centipede slashed and gnashed, allowing none of its human antagonists to escape.

Bisected at the waist, Carden blinked in amazement until her gaze froze.

It was over in a matter of moments.

13

When the news crew from KASO arrived, there was nothing alive in sight and it looked like a string of railroad cars were laying on their side along US-180. But when the chopper lowered and hovered, the producer looked closer and said, "There's no railroad tracks out here." Then, his eyes widened. The railroad cars rose up, and the giant centipede seized one of the copter's landing skids and began pulling it down.

The chopper tipped sideways. The copter blades sliced through the centipede's black, pus-filled abdominal sections and the Devil Head fell, dragging the copter down with it. The resulting explosion, expanded by the chopper fuel, ignited the cruisers as well. Everything was aflame in seconds. The flames licked at the *Scolopendra Heros'* massive carcass, and almost reduced everything to ash.

The Guadalupe Mountains National Park ranger who reported the strange sights at the scene of the incident the next day was never seen or heard from again. Federal authorities were at the site almost simultaneously and had the bizarre "shoot-out" solved in a matter of hours.

Cartel violence.

Multiple casualties, including an El Paso news crew and a female college professor who was taken as a hostage, all deceased.

The men in black cleaned it up, and plans for a second low-level nuclear waste dump near Kent were finalized within months.

Van Horn did, however, get a new football field.

On the absolute, clockwork instant of the commencement of the year 3023, two doors opened at one of the northernmost peaks of the Sierra Diablo Mountain Range, and the metallic cuckoo of the Clock of the Long Now appeared to announce the occasion. No human beings were around to witness it, but there were some *Scolopendra Heros* specimens. With food sources scarce, they had grown much smaller in the long interim.

On the absolute, clockwork instant of the commencement of the year 12023, two doors opened at one of the northernmost peaks of the Sierra Diablo Mountain Range, and the squeaky metallic cuckoo of the Clock of the Long Now appeared one last time to announce the occasion. By then, there were less *Scolopendra Heros* specimens around, but a smattering of diminutive mammals, including small humanoid primates.

The strange magical event was noted by only a few, but it would reverberate in their collective consciousness for hundreds of generations to come.

b-side

Opening Day

Cody Dilworth studied himself in front of his bathroom mirror. The mirror needed to be cleaned, but he didn't notice. His chest hair was coming in strong. He wasn't the dweeby, fat-faced seventeen-year-old who couldn't get a date anymore. He was no longer the JV football player that never made it to varsity. And he wasn't the awkward young man who the niggers and the spicks and faggots were allowed to blame for all their problems. He was a proud, white, twenty-one-year-old American male, the gold standard of the planet. And that finally meant something again.

It was Opening Day, and Dilworth was eager to get to Austin or Houston, he couldn't decide which. Targets would be plentiful in either, but he suspected there would be crowds. He didn't want to get caught in a traffic jam or arrive at a target-rich locale that was already played out.

He needed to leave early, but he wanted to look his best. There would obviously be iPhones, but there might also be television cameras.

When Dilworth held in his stomach, he no longer looked dumpy. And with the military-style semiautomatic rifle strapped across his chest, he looked cool. In fact, he felt like a badass.

Dilworth lived in Atlanta, Texas, where, as he put it, "celebrity Lesbo" Ellen DeGeneres graduated in 1976. The town, situated on the northeastern edge of the Texas-Louisiana asscrack, rarely claimed her, and, of course, the best places to hunt dykes *like* her were hours away. He'd applied for his license and permit, and he had two kill tags, one his and one his friend Jose's. But Jose wasn't able to join him.

"Bitch," Dilworth said, as he recalled his buddy's bad news.

"She doesn't think it's a good idea," Jose had said. "And she thinks it's wrong—to murder . . ."

"Fuck her," Dilworth interrupted. "That's ridiculous. If it was illegal they wouldn't issue us licenses to do it."

"It's just how she feels," Jose replied. "Sorry, man."

"That's why I'm no longer married," Dilworth said. "And no telling what that whore ex-wife of mine is telling my boy. It's fucking bullshit. We're not even allowed to be men anymore."

"I hear ya," Jose replied.

It pissed Cody off. To his way of thinking, Trump's first presidency hadn't been about making America great again so much as making America *America* again. And the man was crucified for it, of course. But the *Demorats'* victory was short-lived. Biden died in office after the midterm elections, and the Republicans impeached Kamala Harris. Then, Trump pulled a Teddy Roosevelt and rewon the presidency.

Straight American white men could breathe again. And the first piece of legislation President Trump signed into law was the Rittenhouse Act. His vice president, former Texas governor Greg Abbott, had proposed the law. Protesters could be fined and imprisoned for exercising yellow-bellied, hippy rights in Texas, and Abbott simply applied it at the Federal level. With the Republicans controlling all three branches of government, the law was expanded and approved almost immediately. And it was simple. The law allowed good, red-blooded American citizens to go out and kill protesters on sight. It was a lot like deer season, except if the families of the deceased transgressors didn't claim their bodies, the carcasses were donated to medical schools or FBI body farms (for decomposition data) instead of transported to meat markets for foodstuff. A new day was dawning in America. And Dilworth wasn't going to miss it.

There was a muted public conniption, of course, but the line the legislation drew was simple. The subversives would no longer be tolerated. Dissent was still every American's right, but every other American had the right to silence it. As Cody's granddad always said, "never let your alligator mouth overload your hummingbird ass." Real Americans were now free to do what they had to do to preserve their heritage and their way of life.

Cody felt good, and the miles were flying by easy. Almost like a countdown. Worst case, he could stop in Dallas, specifically South Dallas. It was full of niggers and they'd no doubt be protesting. "And looting," he said to himself. "Destroying other people's property."

It steamed Cody's ass. He hadn't finished paying off his truck or the credit card he'd used to buy his guns and ammo, so he didn't technically own anything yet. But he would. And when he did, he wanted his property and his rights protected from looters.

Some of his friends from the local gun range had chartered a bus, but Dilworth preferred the lone gunman approach. *Die Hard*. Clint Eastwood's *Dirty Harry*. *The Punisher*. Especially The Punisher. All the faggot liberals needed to be put in their place. The good guys were in charge, again, and there wasn't just a new sheriff in town. The town itself was a sheriff, and the Antifa asshats had better watch out. Slutty women killing their unborn babies was no longer legal, and now looting, Commie arsonists had a target on their backs. "*Yippee-Ki-Yay*, you motherfuckers," Cody said, smiling.

No.

He wasn't going to settle for Dallas. He was going to go for Austin. He put the pedal to the medal and sped up. He would jump to State Hwy 95 in Temple and head south. Then, he would take a right on 290 at Elgin. He would sneak in a side door. He would avoid a lot of the traffic and arrive just after lunch. And if he couldn't find any protesters, he would settle for the stinking parasites in the homeless camps. He could hardly wait. Of course, a homeless person was more like a doe than a real buck, but he would hit his tag limit one way or another. It was a historic day, and he wasn't going to miss out.

The decision pleased him. A friend of his had been at UT when open carry was made legal, and he recalled the stories he'd heard about the Antifa assholes there who had mocked his buddy and others by carrying dildos in holsters on their hips to make fun. Dilworth wished he had been there. He wished the Rittenhouse Act had been in effect then. He would try to get as close to the university as possible.

"Fucking bastards," Dilworth mumbled. "That's what Opening Day of *queer* season is all about."

Dilworth arrived in Austin around 1:30 pm and parked just off the 41st block of Avenue A around 2 o'clock. There were some large, well-kept older houses and a small, newer apartment complex, but the street was empty except for a small group of hunters coming from the south. As he geared up, they grew closer. It was three combat-appareled chicks, around his age. He couldn't believe his luck. Maybe he'd even get laid.

The girls were dressed to the nines. Camo-pants, vintage MAGA hats, tactical vests (that barely covered their bikini-clad tits) and headsets to communicate. They weren't messing around. The girls were all carrying modified AK47s, extra ammo cartridges and knife sheath straps on their thighs. Big ones, fitted for Bowie knives. How awesome was that? It was coming together, and he was stoked.

"Don't you know this town is for pussies?" the closest girl said.

"What I heard," Dilworth said, grinning. "But that's what we're here to fix, right?"

"Fucking A," the girl said. "I'm Carrie."

"I'm Cody," Dilworth replied. "Pleased to meet y'all. Any action yet?"

The girl on the far right held up a wad of dishwater blonde dreadlocks. "I dropped a shithead stoner out of a covey of protesters down on 25th Street an hour or so back," she said. "Name's Jamie."

"I think they know we ain't playing," Carrie added. "It's been a click or two since we've even seen anybody besides you on the streets."

"I hope I didn't get here too late," Dilworth said, but he could hear screaming and gunshots in the distance.

"It's not over, yet," Jamie said. "They were shitting their pants at first. I don't think they thought we were serious. But I'm sure they're just reconnoitering. This is Austin. They got balls, I'll give them that."

"More balls than brains," Dilworth said. "Can I join your party?"

"You bet," Carrie replied. "The more the merrier."

They started moving south and Dilworth took up the rear. The girls seemed to know what they were doing, and he certainly didn't mind having their asses in full view. Jamie was a tall, slender brunette, and Carrie was a shorter blonde with nice curves. Dilworth liked them with meat on their bones, and Carrie's ass filled her camos perfectly. He wished he'd brought a headset, so he could synch up with them.

The other girl, who hadn't said much, looked Italian or Hispanic. She was shorter than Jamie and skinnier than Carrie. But she was all business, minding the gaps between houses and progressing forward carefully. Dilworth figured she was probably the Alpha of the group, at least until he arrived. But it was their detail for now. He knew he would be ready when the time came.

Dilworth's adrenaline was pumping and he felt incredible. He was in the shit! He was on maneuvers with three fucking babes! Jose would never believe it and he would regret the hell out of not coming. It occurred to him that he should take a selfie.

They had already cleared three blocks, and Dilworth was impressed by their knowledge of tactical assault protocol. But all they saw was an abandoned mountain bike. He imagined the shit-scared owner ditching it and trying to run away. He grinned, again.

After a moment, the Alpha girl stopped. Carrie turned and waved him up. "Maria's hearing some chatter about some suspicious activity in the next alley over. You want to take point?"

"Sure," Dilworth replied. "Hell, yeah."

Dilworth stepped up and Maria pointed four fingers left, twice. He nodded and turned left, walking ahead. The girls followed. The alley was a half a block down and, when he got to it, he looked back. Maria thumbed right. Cody held his AK up to his shoulder and scanned left and right before he proceeded. He waved the girls forward without looking over his shoulder. He wondered if it wasn't the coolest thing he'd ever done.

Dilworth moved slowly with an eye out for movement and targets. There were two larger, two-story houses coming up on his left, and they limited the sunlight. It was shady and the perfect place for hippies or hipsters to hide. The girls were close behind him now, and he felt like a man. A real man. He should be in front, he thought. Tip of the fucking spear.

When the group stepped into the deepest shade of the larger of the two houses, Dilworth heard a low hum and Carrie called his name. When he stopped and looked back, Maria, who had moved in closer to him, swung her arm with the low-to-high trajectory of a sucker-punch and stabbed him in his right eye socket. It happened so fast he couldn't even process it, and he stood there, shocked, a flesh-colored, plastic dildo stuck in his head. The sharp, vibrating pain was blinding, and he dropped his AK.

As Dilworth reached up to remove the dildo from his right eye socket, Jamie pulled a plastic dildo from her Bowie knife sheath and stabbed him in the left eye socket, flicking it on as she released it. Cody dropped to his knees and began to scream and whimper. He didn't know what was happening. He called for Carrie, but he didn't hear anything. There was a deafening, vibrating blindness in his head, and he was completely disoriented. He suddenly felt nauseous. He began to vomit and fell forward, catching himself with his elbows. Sounds were barely audible. He sensed snickers and taunts and wondered if there weren't more people around him now, men, women, even children.

Where was his support?

"Medic," he yelled. *"Medic!"*

He felt weak, but he began to crawl forward slowly. The vibrating blackness had almost completely engulfed him, but he could hear voices.

"Let's go, Brandon," someone teased. Then someone cut his belt loose and he thought he felt a hand in his left pocket. He wondered if someone was trying to steal his wallet, but he kept crawling.

Then, he stopped. He carefully, gingerly pulled a bloody dildo out of his left eye socket, and it was still vibrating in his hand. He flung it away shaking, and when he replaced his hand on the pavement, he felt something. It was a gun.

He crawled forward a smidgen and used both hands to feel along the gun, the barrel, the lower handguard.

It was his AK!

But they had removed the magazine.

"Motherfuckers," he grumbled, but he knew something that they didn't. They'd removed his main magazine and his spare, but he had another strapped to his left ankle.

He rolled over on his back. The smell of his own blood enraged him, but he kept his cool. He slowly, and carefully removed the second dildo from his right eye socket. He could feel the blood streaming down his cheeks, but it slicked his socket for the delicate extraction.

Dilworth gritted his teeth, removed the magazine from his left ankle and jammed it in his AK.

He wasn't sure exactly what had happened, and he didn't know what was going on, but knew those goddamn hippy chicks made a big mistake. They left him alive.

Dilworth couldn't see and he couldn't think straight, but he could still stand and shoot.

Locked and loaded, he began firing as he spun, pointing his gun in every direction and at every level. He would die with his boots on. He would shoot anything and everything around him.

They would all pay.

Everyone would pay.

AUTHOR

E. R. Bills is an award-winning author and freelance journalist. His fiction work includes *Pendulum Grim* (2020) and he was the co-creator and is the current executive editor of the annual *Road Kill: Texas Horror by Texas Writers*, the first anthology of Texas horror, featuring works from Joe. R. Lansdale, Stephen Graham Jones, Robert E. Howard, Katherine Anne Porter, O. Henry, David Bowles, etc. His horror fiction has been compared to that of Stephen King, Ray Bradbury, Richard Matheson, Matt Shaw, Theodore Sturgeon and others.

Bills' nonfiction works include *Texas Obscurities: Stories of the Peculiar, Exceptional and Nefarious* (2013), *The 1910 Slocum Massacre: An Act of Genocide in East Texas* (2014), *Texas Far and Wide: The Tornado with Eyes, Gettysburg's Last Casualty, the Celestial Skipping Stone and Other Tales* (2017), *Texas Oblivion:*

Mysterious Disappearances, Escapes and Cover-Ups (2021) *100 Things to Do in Texas Before You Die* (2022) and the upcoming *Tell-Tale Texas: Investigations into Infamous History* (2023).

Bills has also written for the *Austin American-Statesman*, the *Fort Worth Star-Telegram*, *Texas Co-Op Power* magazine, *Fort Worth Magazine* and *Fort Worth Weekly*. He currently lives in North Texas with his wife, Stacie.

STARKWEATHER
IMPRINTS